Fall Leaf Project

Written by Margaret McNamara
Illustrated by Mike Gordon

Ready-to-Read

SCHOLASTIC INC.
New York Toronto London Auckland Sydney
Mexico City New Delhi Hong Kong Buenos Aires

For Barbara Bowen, a born teacher

ISBN-13: 978-0-439-91515-1
ISBN-10: 0-439-91515-5

Text copyright © 2006 by Brenda Bowen.
Illustrations copyright © 2006 by Mike Gordon. All rights reserved.
Published by Scholastic Inc., 557 Broadway, New York, NY 10012, by arrangement with Aladdin Paperbacks, an imprint of Simon & Schuster Children's Publishing Division. SCHOLASTIC and associated logos are trademarks and/or registered trademarks of Scholastic Inc.
READY-TO-READ is a registered trademark of Simon & Schuster, Inc.

12 11 10 9 8 7 6 5 4   7 8 9 10 11/0

Printed in the U.S.A.   23

First Scholastic printing, October 2006

Designed by Sammy Yuen Jr.

The text of this book was set in Century Schoolbook.

Mrs. Connor's class
was learning about fall.
Mrs. Connor showed
the class a map.

"In our state," she said,
"leaves change color.

In other states,
they do not."

"Oh, no!" said Emma.

"We have so many
fall leaves,"
said Hannah.
"Can we share them?"

"Good idea,"
said Mrs. Connor.
"I know a teacher
in a state where the leaves
do not change.

His name is Mr. Soto.
We can send leaves
to his class."

Mrs. Connor's class
went outside.

"Gather your favorite leaves," said Mrs. Connor.

Kate chose seven
yellow leaves.

Ayanna chose nine
orange leaves.

Jamie liked red leaves
the best.
He chose eleven of them.

"Watch me!" said Michael.
Michael jumped into
a great big pile
of leaves.

Becky, Emma, and Hannah
sorted the leaves
they found.
"Oak, oak, oak,"
said Hannah.

"Maple, maple," said Becky.

"Chestnut," said Emma.

"What is this one?"
asked Hannah.
It looked like a mitten.
"That is sassafras!"
said Mrs. Connor.

Back in the classroom,
the first-graders
got to work.
Nia wrote.

Reza glued.

Eigen wrapped.

Mrs. Connor packed.

Hannah licked the stamps.

"There," said Mrs. Connor.
"Our project is done."

Three days later
Mr. Soto's first-graders
opened the package.

They decorated
their classroom
with the leaves.

They sent a letter
to Mrs. Connor's class.

Dear First-Graders
of Robin Hill School,
Thank you for the leaves.

We love the colors.
We love the shapes.
Your friends,
Mr. Soto's First-Graders

P.S. Happy fall!